Pinocchio

Carlo Collodi

Retold by Katie Daynes

Illustrated by
Mauro Evangelista

Reading Consultant: Alison Kelly
University of Surrey Roehampton

Contents

Chapter 1

A piece of wood

Once upon a time there was... a piece of wood. Lying in a corner of the carpenter's workshop, it looked just like any other piece of wood. The carpenter's name was Mr. Cherry and he needed a table leg.

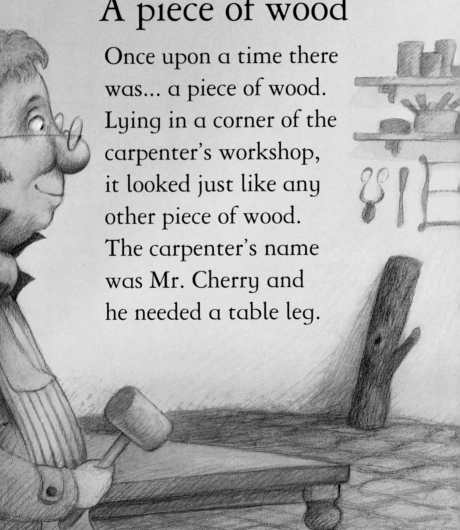

"Perfect!" he said, catching sight of the wood. He rested it against his worktop and picked up a chisel.

As the chisel touched the wood, a voice cried out, "Don't hurt me!"

Mr. Cherry looked up in surprise. He was alone in the room. "I must be imagining things," he thought.

But when he tried again, tapping the chisel against the wood, someone screamed.

"Who's there?" shouted Mr. Cherry. There was no answer.

Wood can't talk, can it?

He shook the wood and listened carefully... nothing. Just then, his friend Gepetto knocked at the door.

"I want to make a puppet," announced Gepetto.

"Good for you, macaroni hair," called a voice.

Gepetto went red in the face and glared at Mr. Cherry. "What did you say?" he shouted.

"It must have been you," said Gepetto. "There's no one else here. But give me some wood and I might forgive you."

Mr. Cherry was happy to get rid of the strange piece of wood. The wood had other ideas and jabbed Gepetto in the tummy.

"How dare you!" Gepetto shouted, almost losing his wig. He grabbed at Mr. Cherry's arm and Mr. Cherry pushed him away.

Biff! went Gepetto, knocking off
Mr. Cherry's wig. *Boff!* went Mr.
Cherry and Gepetto's wig fell to
the floor.

After that, the two men looked so
silly, they burst out laughing. And
then they weren't cross any more.

"Goodbye, my friend," said
Gepetto, taking the piece of wood.

"Goodbye, Gepetto," replied Mr.
Cherry. He closed the door and
breathed a sigh of relief.

Chapter 2

Puppet trouble

Gepetto strolled home clutching his piece of wood. "I'll make the best puppet in the world," he thought, "and call him... Pinocchio."

First, he chipped at the wood to
make a head with
hair. Then he
gave the puppet
two eyes. No
sooner were they
finished than one
of them winked.

Gepetto didn't notice. He had
moved on to the puppet's nose. As

he smoothed it
down, the nose
began to grow.
Every time he
chopped it off,
it grew again,
longer and
longer.

Gepetto gave up on the ridiculous

nose and carved out a mouth. Before he'd even finished, the mouth laughed.

"What's so funny?" asked Gepetto. Instead of replying, the puppet stuck out its tongue.

"Behave!" said Gepetto, shaping the puppet's body. "Remember, you're only a piece of wood."

11

But when the legs and arms were finished, a hand reached out and snatched Gepetto's wig. Before he could say, "Stop Pinocchio!" the puppet jumped up and ran out of the house...

Wait!

...slap bang into a policeman.

"What's going on here?" asked the policeman. Then he saw Gepetto, waving his chisel, and decided he looked dangerous.

"You're under arrest for threatening a puppet," the policeman said, leading Gepetto away.

13

Chapter 3

Fire!

Pinocchio skipped merrily
back to Gepetto's house.

"How nice to be all by
myself," he said, grinning.

"Cri cri cri, what about me?"
buzzed a cricket.

"Buzz off!" cried Pinocchio.

But the cricket had a lot to say. He told Pinocchio to respect his father. "Only good sons have a chance of becoming *real* boys. And real boys are better than puppets."

Pinocchio didn't like this bossy cricket. He covered his ears, but the cricket kept buzzing. "Shut up, or I'll squash you!" he cried.

15

"A bad temper will get you nowhere," answered the cricket.

By this time, Pinocchio was very annoyed. He picked up a hammer and threw it at the wall.

"Oh no!" cried Pinocchio. "I didn't mean to hit you!"

The cricket couldn't reply. He was a flattened blob on the wall. Pinocchio felt very guilty for a while. Then he felt hungry.

Searching through the kitchen cupboards, the only food he found was an egg. He cracked it open on the side of a frying pan.

But instead of runny egg slipping into the pan, a chick flew into the air. "Thank you for freeing me," she twittered and disappeared out of the window.

Now there was nothing to eat.
Poor Pinocchio was cold, tired and
absolutely starving. He settled in
the armchair, rested his legs on
the fireplace and fell asleep.

A knock at the door woke
Pinocchio with a jolt. There was
smoke all around him. He jumped
up – and fell down with a bump.
The fire had burned off his feet.

"Let me in," called Gepetto.

"I can't walk!" cried Pinocchio.

Gepetto thought the puppet was just being lazy, so he climbed in through the window.

"Oh my poor boy," he gasped, seeing Pinocchio on the floor. He forgot all about his cold night in a prison cell and rushed to help his puppet son.

Chapter 4

A puppet show

With a new pair of feet and a full stomach, Pinocchio was a much happier puppet. "Gepetto," he said, "you're a great Dad and I've been a rotten son, but I promise to be good from now on."

Gepetto chuckled. "Really?"

"Well..." said Pinocchio, "it might be easier if I was a real boy."

"I see," replied Gepetto. "Then let's start by sending you to school."

Pinocchio frowned. He didn't like the idea of school.

All boys go to school.

That afternoon, Gepetto sold his only coat to buy his son a school book and some clothes.

In the morning, Pinocchio forced himself to smile at Gepetto as he left for his first day at school.

On the way, he noticed a crowd of people. They were standing outside a brightly painted building.

"What's going on?" he asked.

"A puppet show!" cried a man. "And it begins in ten minutes."

Pinocchio knew he should go to school, but he was longing to see a puppet show.

"I'll go to school tomorrow," he thought, and joined the crowd. When he realized he needed money for a ticket, he almost cried.

"Give me that nice, new book and I'll let you in," said the ticketmaster.

Pinocchio thought of his poor Dad selling his only coat for the book. Then he thought of a real, live puppet show. "OK!" he said, and raced in.

On stage stood the famous puppets, Harlequin and Punchinello. Their dances and tricks made the audience howl with laughter.

All of a sudden, the puppets stopped acting and stared into the crowd.

"Another puppet!" they cried.
"Come up and join us."

Pinocchio was dragged on stage and surrounded by puppets. They chattered about this and that and completely forgot their show. The people in the audience grew angry and frustrated.

Who's he?

Get on with the show!

Then a scary man stormed onto the stage and everyone fell silent. It was the manager, a fearsome fire-eater. He grabbed the puppets and marched them off.

Backstage, the fire-eater looked sternly at a trembling Pinocchio. "You've ruined my show, puppet!" he yelled. "Now I'm going to use you for firewood."

"Don't burn me," begged
Pinocchio, "I don't want to die.
How would my poor old Dad cope
without me?"

"Ah... ah... ah-tishoo!" sneezed
the fire-eater.

The other puppets cheered.
"A sneeze means he feels
sorry for you,"
they cried.

"Take these five gold coins back
home to your father," said the fire-
eater, "and stay out of trouble!"

Chapter 5

The fox and the cat

Lucky Pinocchio waved goodbye to his puppet friends and skipped off down the road. He was dreaming of what Gepetto could buy with the gold coins, when he bumped into a fox and a cat.

They were a sorry sight. The fox was lame and had to lean on the cat. The cat was blind and had to be led by the fox.

"What are you smiling about, young puppet?" asked the fox.

"I'm rich," replied Pinocchio. "And my Dad will be so pleased with me."

At the word *rich*, the cat looked
up. The fox kicked her with his
lame leg and she quickly shut
her eyes.

"Why not double your money?"
suggested the cat.

"Or triple it!" added the fox.

Pinocchio was confused. "How do
I do that?" he asked.

"Come with us to the field of
miracles," replied the cat.

Pinocchio pictured himself carrying home bags of gold. "Dad will be thrilled," he cried and followed his new friends out of town.

Just before sunset, they stopped at an inn. The fox and cat ordered everything on the menu, but Pinocchio was too excited to eat.

"Let's sleep here a while," said the cat, showing Pinocchio to the guest rooms.

As soon as Pinocchio's head hit the pillow, he drifted off into a wonderful dream. Everywhere he looked, gold grew on trees.

"Wake up!" called a grumpy voice. "Your friends have gone without you and they haven't paid."

Pinocchio rubbed his eyes. It was the innkeeper. Handing him a gold coin, Pinocchio rushed outside.

The puppet stumbled blindly in the dark. His only thought was to find the fox and cat.

"Foolish puppet," buzzed a faint but familiar voice.

"Who said that?" whispered Pinocchio.

I am the ghost of the cricket. Now take those coins home.

"Leave me alone," Pinocchio cried. "I'm going to triple my money at the field of miracles!"

"There's no such place," said the cricket. "This lane will only take you to madmen and murderers."

"They don't scare *me*," sniffed Pinocchio. Turning his back on the cricket, he stomped off into the gloom.

Slowly, the moon slipped out
from behind a cloud and
spread a ghostly glow
across the lane. Ahead,
Pinocchio could just
make out two figures.
They looked like...
murderers.

Quickly, Pinocchio hid.

"We can see you, puppet," snarled one of the murderers.

"Bring us your gold," purred the other.

A paw brushed past Pinocchio's cheek, so Pinocchio snapped at it – and bit it off!

By kicking, scratching and biting, Pinocchio managed to escape. He fled through the woods, but the murderers sped after him.

Fighting his way through the thick trees, he finally came out into a clearing.

Chapter 6

Meeting a fairy

Up ahead, Pinocchio saw a little cottage. He banged his wooden fists against the door and shouted for help.

Poor Pinocchio could still hear the patter of murderous feet. "HELP!" he shouted again.

A light went on and the front door swung open. The frightened puppet was invited in by a very polite poodle.

"My lady is sleeping," he said, "but do come in. I'll show you to your room."

Relieved to escape certain death, Pinocchio followed him.

"You may sleep here, Master Pinocchio," said the poodle. "Breakfast will be served at eight."

Pinocchio was so pleased to be safe, he didn't stop to wonder how the poodle knew his name.

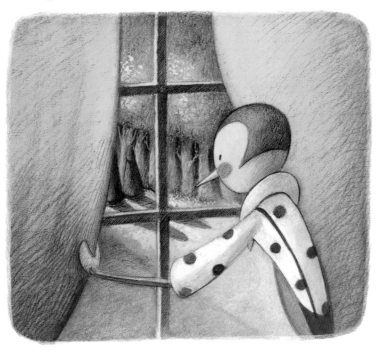

At breakfast, Pinocchio met the lady of the house. She was a silvery fairy who twinkled like starlight. Pinocchio told her about his adventure, from the fire-eater and the gold coins to the murderers in the woods.

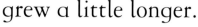

"And where are your coins now?" she asked. "Can I see them?"

"No!" said Pinocchio quickly. "Because I've... er... lost them." As the words left his mouth, his nose grew a little longer.

"Where did you lose them?" asked the fairy, smiling.

"Um... in the woods," lied the puppet. Instantly, his nose doubled in length. "Or maybe I swallowed them," he added. By now, his nose was touching the wall – and the coins were jangling in his pocket.

"You're lying," giggled the fairy.

You'll never be a real boy if you don't tell the truth.

Pinocchio felt very awkward. He tried to run from the room, but his incredibly long nose got in the way.

Soon the fairy stopped laughing and took pity on him. She opened the window and called for three woodpeckers. In no time, they had pecked Pinocchio's nose back to its original size.

A woodpecker whispered something in the fairy's ear.

"Good news!" cried the fairy, turning to Pinocchio. "Your father is in these woods looking for you."

Pinocchio jumped for joy. "I must go and greet him," he cried.

"And give him those coins," added the fairy, pointing to his pocket.

With a sheepish grin, Pinocchio raced outside.

45

Chapter 7

The field of miracles

Before Pinocchio could find Gepetto, who should he bump into but the fox and cat? They were very friendly and apologized for leaving him at the inn.

"Now let's go to the field of miracles!" said the sly fox.

"Not me," said Pinocchio. "I'm off to find my Dad."

"With only four coins in your pocket?" said the cat.

"What a shame," added the fox, "when you could have twenty."

"No! I've made up my mind," said the puppet. "Goodbye."

"Goodbye," called the fox and cat. "See you when we're rich!"

Pinocchio turned to
leave, then remembered
his dream of golden
trees. "Wait for me!"
he cried.

But the field of miracles was
nothing like Pinocchio's dream. It
looked just like any other field.

"You must bury your gold in the middle of the field," said the fox.

"Then take this pebble and throw it in the river," said the cat. "When you come back, your gold will have multiplied."

Oh no it won't!

Pinocchio eagerly dug a hole. He covered the coins with mud, then ran down to the river.

When he got back, the fox and cat had disappeared. He rushed to the middle of the field and dug.

"Silly puppet!" squawked a parrot. "Did you really believe their story?"

Pinocchio ignored him and dug deeper and deeper, until he was covered in dirt. The only thing he found was a worm.

I've been tricked!

Chapter 8

Toyland

For hours, Pinocchio sulked in the field. When a huge pigeon called out to him, he didn't bother replying.

"Pinocchio?" cooed the pigeon again.

Pinocchio just sniffed.

"Gepetto is in great danger," the pigeon went on. "Come quickly."

Before Pinocchio could reply, the pigeon scooped him onto her back and soared into the sky. They darted through clouds and arrived at the seashore, just as a huge storm blew up.

A huddle of people stood on the shore. They were pointing to a small boat struggling in the rough sea.

"That poor man," said a woman. "He can't even swim!"

"He only wanted to find his son," sighed another. Suddenly, a huge wave swamped the little boat.

"Dad?" cried Pinocchio. "If I was a good son, you wouldn't be in danger." Then he dived into the frothy water.

Pinocchio swam and swam. Soon the storm died down, but there was still no sign of Gepetto's boat. The wet, miserable puppet was washed onto a sandy beach.

He heard whoops of laughter, then a gang of toys appeared.

"Welcome to Toyland," called a tin soldier.

"Here we only have fun, fun and more fun!" cried a Jack-in-the-box.

54

"I don't want fun," groaned Pinocchio. "My Dad has just drowned and it's all my fault."

"We'll cheer you up!" shouted the toys.

"Watch out," said a twinkling voice. "They'll make a fool of you."

Pinocchio looked up, hoping to see the fairy. All he could see were grinning toys.

Over the next few days,
Pinocchio tried very hard not to
have fun. But there was so much to
do. The island was one big funfair,
with free rides all day long.

"Whoopee!" cried Pinocchio,
zooming through the air on a
rollercoaster.

"Look at me!" he shouted,
bouncing higher on
a trampoline.

In all the excitement, he
completely forgot about Gepetto.
"You silly wooden toy," said the
fairy voice one afternoon. "You're
no better than a donkey."
This time, Pinocchio ignored her.
What did she know about fun?

The next morning, Pinocchio woke up feeling itchy all over. His ears were unusually heavy and he was growing fur. Nervously, he looked in the mirror. "Oh no!" he cried. He was turning into a donkey.

He couldn't let anyone see him like this. Without a second thought, he ran to the beach, jumped into the sea and swam away.

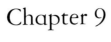

Chapter 9

Inside the shark

It was hard for Pinocchio
to swim as a donkey. He
felt very heavy and little
fish kept tugging on his
coat. Then he realized they
were nibbling off his fur.

Soon Pinocchio was a puppet once more. But as he swam to shore, a shark the size of an ocean liner rose above the waves. There was a tremendous WHOOSH, then everything went dark.

Eventually, Pinocchio saw a faint glow in the distance. The glow led him to a man reading by candlelight.

"Dad?" whispered the puppet, hardly daring to believe his eyes. "Pinocchio!" cried Gepetto.

The old man had survived for weeks on food supplies from a ship the shark had swallowed. But now the food had run out. "We're doomed, my son," Gepetto sighed.

"This is all my fault," cried Pinocchio. "If I was a *real* boy, I'd get us out of here." He grabbed Gepetto's hand. "It's OK," he declared. "I'll *still* get us out."

He led Gepetto on a squelchy journey to the shark's mouth, where their exit was barred by teeth.

Suddenly, the shark let out a giant burp, throwing Pinocchio and Gepetto into the sea.

The brave puppet towed Gepetto to the shore and, by dusk, they were home again.

That night, the fairy appeared to Pinocchio in a dream. "Well done," she said and kissed him.

Pinocchio woke up in surprise. He rubbed his eyes – and was even more surprised. His hands weren't wooden any more!

Hearing him shout, Gepetto ran into the room. "Son," he cried with joy, "you're a real boy at last!"

Carlo Collodi (1826-1890) was an Italian writer and a schools' advisor. His real name was Carlo Lorenzini but he used Collodi as his writing name, after the village Collodi where he was born.

Series editor: Lesley Sims

Designed by Russell Punter
and Katarina Dragoslavic

First published in 2004 by Usborne Publishing Ltd., Usborne House, 83-85 Saffron Hill, London EC1N 8RT, England. www.usborne.com
Copyright © 2004 Usborne Publishing Ltd.